## DEDICATION

*To my agent, Harvey Unna –*
*the original Harvey who gave me the idea,*
*as noble and sagacious as his namesake.*

# HARVEY
## TO THE RESCUE

### TERRANCE DICKS

ORCHARD BOOKS

ORCHARD BOOKS
96 Leonard Street, London EC2A 4RH
*Orchard Books Australia*
14 Mars Road, Lane Cove, NSW 2066
ISBN 1 86039  343 8 (paperback)
First published in Great Britain by Piccadilly Press Ltd
1995
First paperback publication 1997
Text © Terrance Dicks 1995
Illustrations © Susan Hellard 1995
A CIP catalogue record for this book is available from the
British Library.
Printed in Great Britain by
The Guernsey Press Co Ltd, Vale, Guernsey, Channel Islands.

*Chapter One*
## Too Late!

When the deep tones of the warning bell rolled through the old Swiss monastery, Harvey was eager to answer the call of duty. (Actually, his real name was 'Herve', but English visitors always pronounced it 'Harvey', and the name had stuck. Even the monks called him Harvey now.)

Even though he was sound asleep in the warm straw, the noble St Bernard still heard the bell. Without a moment's hesitation, he squeezed out of his kennel, and lolloped along the stone corridors to the monastery kitchen.

There he found tubby little Brother Martin, bustling around the old-fashioned stove, heating up a bubbling pot of soup, and cutting great slices of warm, freshly-baked bread.

"Aha, my good Harvey!" said the little monk. "As always, you hear the bell. Somewhere there are poor people lost in the snow – injured, perhaps. By the time they are rescued and brought back here there will be my good hot soup all ready for them."

"Woof!" said Harvey. The deep, crashing bark echoed round the big kitchen.

"Never fear, all will be ready."

"WOOF!" said Harvey again, much louder. He went over to a cupboard in the corner and opened it with one big paw.

Brother Martin sighed. "But that is no

longer necessary."

"WOOF!" said the big dog, giving the loudest bark of all.

He took Brother Martin by the edge of the apron and tugged him gently over to the cupboard.

"Very well," said Brother Martin. "If you insist – and I see that you do!"

From out of the cupboard he took a little wooden barrel, with a harness arrangement of leather straps. He shook the barrel.

"You see, Harvey? It is still full of brandy from last time."

Ignoring him, the St Bernard bounded up eagerly and sat down. With a sigh, the little monk fastened the harness around his friend's big chest. He stepped back, checking that everything was in order. There was a little tap at the bottom of the barrel, and a little cup

suspended on a long chain.

When the St Bernard dug some stranded traveller out of the snow, it was quite easy for the traveller to get hold of the cup, turn the little tap, and pour himself a reviving tot of brandy. Or even two or three tots. Strictly for medicinal purposes of course. (Some snowbound travellers had been known to say they didn't care how long it took the rescuers to arrive.)

When everything was properly in place, Harvey gave Brother Martin a "Woof" of thanks and bounded out of the kitchen, heading for the big front door. He barked until Brother Gerard, the old gatekeeper, appeared.

Brother Gerard, who was tall and thin, sighed just like Brother Martin. "Oh Harvey, not again!"

"Woof!" said Harvey firmly.

Brother Gerard opened the door and soon Harvey was rushing down the path.

The old monastery stood on a mountain top, surrounded by steeply sloping fields of snow. Far below, at the very bottom of the mountain, twinkled the lights of the little town.

It was easy to guess where the stranded skiers were. Over to the left were the steeper, more dangerous mountain slopes. There were always some daring skiers who wanted to ski on them – and they were usually the ones who ended up in trouble.

It was getting dark now, and Harvey saw a little cluster of lights in the snow, way over to the left. He was a little disappointed not to be the first – but surely there must be some poor cold people out there who needed a little nip of brandy.

Harvey bounded happily over the snow. As he got closer, he saw that the skiers and their rescuers were gathered at the top of a little rise. He had almost reached them when something big and white and noisy soared over the rise. It hung suspended a few feet from the ground as the rescue team helped the skiers inside and scrambled in after them. Just as Harvey reached the top of the rise, the helicopter rose and floated away. He was too late.

Harvey looked on sadly as the helicopter whisked away the injured skier. He sat down in the snow, feeling the weight of the brandy round his neck.

"I'm useless," he thought. "They just don't need me any more."

Sadly, Harvey turned and began the long climb back up to the monastery. By the time he arrived the helicopter was parked on the monastery forecourt.

When he reached the kitchen it was full of happy laughing people, drinking Brother Martin's hot soup.

They all cheered when Harvey appeared in the doorway, the useless barrel of brandy around his neck.

They cheered – and they laughed as well.

"Come on Harvey old fellow," someone shouted. "Large brandies all round!"

Ignoring him, Harvey walked over to Brother Martin, and waited patiently while the little barrel was unfastened from around his neck. He watched sadly while the barrel and its harness were stowed away in the corner cupboard.

Old Pierre, the mountain guide and head of the rescue team, came over and stroked his head.

"My poor Harvey," he said, "like me, you miss the old days. The rescue bell sounds and we all set off to seek the poor snowbound traveller. The brave St Bernard goes ahead, his little barrel around his neck. Always he finds the buried traveller first, sniffing him out with his wonderful nose! He digs him out of the snow with his paws. He gives him brandy, saving his life, and then barks to bring the rest of us to the rescue. Then we load the poor fellow on a stretcher, and carry him home."

Old Pierre looked deep into Harvey's sad brown eyes.

"Now everything is different," he whispered. He looked at the rescued skiers.

"Today the fools carry little telephones! If they get in trouble, they call us up, we radio the heliport, we pick them up and poof! It is all over." He patted Harvey's head.

"To be honest, my brave Harvey, the modern way is better. Sometimes you know, in the old days, we arrived too late. By the time we found the poor traveller, not even your brandy could do him any good." He sighed. "Oh, the modern way is better – but it's not nearly as much fun! Especially for you, my poor Harvey..."

Harvey sighed too, and went sadly back to his kennel.

## Chapter Two
### HARVEY'S SEARCH

A few days later, Brother Martin went to
see the Prior, the wise old monk who was
in charge of the monastery.

"I'm very worried about Harvey. He
just lies in his kennel, head on his paws,
staring into space. I'm beginning to wonder if he's ill."

"I've been worrying about Harvey
myself," said the Prior. "I shall go and
talk to him at once."

The Prior made his way to Harvey's

kennel, which stood in the great hall beside the main door. Harvey was lying in the kennel, head on paws, just as Brother Martin had said.

Usually when he saw the Prior, Harvey jumped up to greet him. This time he could only manage a couple of thumps with his tail.

"Harvey, old friend, it's time we had a little talk," said the Prior. "Come on out of there, we'll go for a walk."

Harvey didn't feel in the least like a walk, but he didn't want to upset the Prior. He crawled out of his kennel and lumbered after him. They walked down the mountain path towards the town, stopping half-way in a meadow full of wild flowers.

"Harvey, I know what's troubling you," said the old Prior.

"You're a Mountain Rescue dog. You were bred for it and trained for it. Now the helicopter has taken over your job. You're not needed anymore. You're out of date."

Harvey hung his head. It was all too true.

"Only it's not true!" said the Prior.

Harvey jerked his head up in surprise.

It wasn't?

"It's all in the way you think about it," said the Prior.

Harvey cocked his head, puzzled.

"Think!" urged the Prior. "What is it you really want to do? Dig people out of snowdrifts and bring them brandy – is that it?"

Harvey nodded eagerly.

"And if you can't do that any more, life's not worth living?"

Harvey nodded again, sadly this time.

"Wrong!" shouted the Prior. "What you really want to do, Harvey, is help people. You need to do something useful. So what do you have to do?"

Harvey gave him a puzzled frown.

"Come on Harvey, you're an intelligent hound. There are all sorts of ways you could help people. You just have to find out what they are."

The Prior leaned forward. "Our monastery will always be your home, Harvey. If you like, you can stay with us for the rest of your life. But if you want to be really happy again, you'll have to go out into the world and find yourself something to do."

The Prior stood up. "I must be getting back to the monastery. Which way are you going, Harvey? Back to your kennel to lie down and brood all day? Or out into the world to start your new life?"

Harvey sat up straight. Raising one massive paw he pointed towards the town.

The Prior took the paw and shook it solemnly. "Goodbye Harvey, and good luck."

He turned away quickly and set off up the road towards the monastery. Harvey watched him go for a moment and then turned and headed down towards the town. His head was up, his tail was held high. He was a dog in search of his destiny...

## Chapter Three
## THE RESCUE

On the terrace of the Edelweiss Cafe, the Smiths were having a family row.

The cafe stood on the last outcrop of the mountain. From its outdoor terrace you could see the whole town laid out below like a model. You could see the red-roofed houses, the trams, and the big hotel. You could see a train drawing into the station. All around the little town there was a ring of snow-capped mountains.

It was a wonderful view but the Smiths weren't getting the benefit of it. They were too busy fighting.

Mrs Smith, a successful business-woman and a born organiser, was sur-rounded by maps and guide books. "We'll go to the Folk Museum first," she said.

"Museums are boring," said Harry. "I want to try ice skating."

"Why can't we all just go skiing again?" said his sister Sally. "I thought we came here to ski."

"Can't we just take it easy?" groaned Mr Smith. He was a civil servant and he liked a quiet life, though he seldom got it.

Buster, their terrible toddler, roared, "Gimme!" He'd finished his orange and was after Sally's coke.

When she snatched it away he kicked her ankle.

"Ouch!" said Sally, and slapped his wrist.

Buster screamed, more with rage than pain, and Mrs Smith said sharply, "Leave him alone, Sally, violence isn't the answer!"

"Tell *him* that," shouted Sally, rubbing her ankle.

"Don't be such a baby, Sally," said Harry. "Never mind, Buster..." He ruffled Buster's hair.

Buster stopped crying and kicked Harry hard on the knee.

"You little beast!" yelled Harry. "I'll get you for that!"

"Don't you kids ever stop fighting?" groaned Mr Smith.

In the middle of the fuss, a big St Bernard dog came on to the terrace. Harvey had decided to stop for a rest and a think.

Leon, the cafe owner, knew Harvey well. "How are you, Harvey? How are all the good monks?"

The noisy quarrelling group on the other side of the terrace caught Harvey's attention. He looked enquiringly at Leon.

Leon shrugged. "Families come here for a happy holiday, and all they do is make each other miserable. I wish I could help..."

The last word caught Harvey's attention. Could he help?

Harvey's chance to help the Smiths arrived right away.

The smallest human wriggled off his chair and staggered across the terrace. The rest of the family were too busy arguing to notice. The terrace was protected from the sheer drop below by a wooden fence. The small human started swarming up it...

Suddenly Mrs Smith realised Buster was no longer in his chair.

She heard a triumphant shout, "Looka Me!"

She turned and saw Buster balanced on top of the fence – with a sheer drop on the other side.

"Buster no!" she screamed. "Don't move!"

Frightened by the panic in his mother's voice, Buster started to cry – and lost his balance.

Just as he started to topple forwards, a huge furry blur flashed across the terrace, and two jaws snapped shut on the baggy seat of Buster's romper suit.

Carrying Buster, much as a mother cat carries a kitten, Harvey trotted across the terrace and dropped the astonished toddler back into his mother's lap.

Mrs Smith grabbed Buster and hugged him. Then, as with many worried parents, relief turned to anger, and she shook him. "Buster, you bad boy!"

Buster started to roar.

"Woof!"

Buster shut up from sheer surprise, and Mrs Smith looked up to see a large and handsome St Bernard dog looking reproachfully at her. She stared into the big brown eyes. The dog seemed to be trying to tell her something...

"It wasn't Buster's fault," she said slowly. "He's too little to be sensible. I should have kept more of an eye on him."

"Woof!" said Harvey again. The great head turned and the sad brown eyes looked round at the rest of the Smith family.

"We've no right to leave it all to mum," said Mr Smith. "We all know how fast

Buster can move and the dangerous things he gets up to... We should all have been looking out for him."

"Only we were too busy fighting," said Harry.

"Sorry Buster," said Sally. She gave him a kiss.

Buster was amazed.

Leon, the cafe owner, had seen what was happening. He rushed over in a panic. "How terrible! Is the little boy all right?"

"How fortunate Harvey was here!"

Mr Smith was still a bit shaken, and just like his wife, his relief turned to anger. "Buster could have been killed! This terrace isn't safe – I shall complain to the police!"

Leon leaped to the defence of his cafe. "You cannot blame me. There is the fence. No normal child would try to climb it!

Only a little monkey."

"Are you calling my child a monkey?" shouted Mrs Smith.

"Woof!" said Harvey loudly. Everyone shut up.

Leon drew a deep breath. "However, it is most regrettable that such a thing should happen. I will have the fence made higher. Please accept your refreshments with the compliments of the management."

The Smiths were delighted. What with the high costs of ski-lifts and ski-hire, they'd been finding the holiday very expensive. They all parted good friends.

As they got up to go, Buster pointed to Harvey. "Ride!"

"No, dear, it's a dog, not a horse."

"Ride, doggy!" roared Buster.

Harvey walked over and stood beside them.

"I think he's saying he doesn't mind," said Sally.

Mrs Smith put Buster on Harvey's back and Buster hung on tight, clenching his little fists in the thick fur.

Harvey moved off the cafe terrace, leading the Smiths to the little funicular railway which ran between the cafe and the town.

When the cable car arrived, Harvey walked inside, with Buster still on his back.

"Looks as if he's adopted us," said Mrs Smith.

"Can we keep him?" asked Harry.

"Yes, please let's," said Sally.

"Keep doggy!" yelled Buster.

"Well, maybe just for a little while," said Mr Smith. "He's not really ours. We must try to get in touch with his owners. We'll ask at the hotel."

"I don't think he's lost at all," said Mrs
Smith. "Something tells me that dog
knows exactly what he's doing!"

Mrs Smith was right. Harvey had come
to a decision.

Looking after the Smith family was
going to be his new job.

## Chapter Four
### HARVEY ON GUARD

As if one new job wasn't enough, Harvey was offered another straight away.

When they all got back to the Hotel Alpine where the Smiths were staying Monsieur Emil, the large and imposing manager, recognised Harvey at once.

"There is no need to worry," he told the Smiths. "Harvey lives up at the monastery, but he often comes to town for a look around. Everyone knows him. I will telephone the Prior and tell him

Harvey is here. Why don't you wait on the hotel terrace while I call?"

They all went and sat on the glassed-in hotel terrace overlooking the busy main street. Gustave, the ancient waiter, tottered over and said, "Bonjour Harvey! The manager would like to offer you and your friends some refreshment."

They ordered coffees and soft drinks and some cakes, and a bowl of water and some dog biscuits for Harvey.

"It's like travelling with royalty, being with Harvey," said Harry as they were all tucking in. "We don't seem to have to pay for anything!"

"Just as well," said Mr Smith. "Everything's so expensive abroad, we're just about going to manage till the end of the holiday. Oh, let me have those travellers cheques will you, dear? I must change the rest of them pretty soon. I'm going to shop around first and see where we get the best exchange rate. Every little helps!"

Mrs Smith took the cheques from her handbag. "You will be careful with them, won't you dear?"

"Of course I will! Honestly, anyone would think I was hopeless."

Mrs Smith sometimes thought her husband was hopeless, or at least hopelessly vague. He'd lost things before. But she didn't like to upset him by saying so. She handed over the travellers cheques.

A tall man in baggy tweeds strolled by just as Mr Smith was putting the travellers cheques in his wallet. He had a red face and a bushy white moustache. "I wouldn't wave those around if I were you, old chap. Not safe, you know – even in a good hotel like this!" He patted Harvey on the head. Harvey put up with

it, but he didn't seem to like it much.

"Your dog? Splendid animal the St Bernard, got a couple myself, at home on the estate." He raised his hat to Mrs Smith and strolled off.

Monsieur Emil arrived as the stranger left, bowing low as he passed. "Bonjour, Milord. Enjoy your stroll!"

He sat down at their table, speaking not to the Smiths but to Harvey. "I have been talking to the Prior, Harvey, and he tells me you are seeking new employment. Perhaps we can help each other."

He looked at the Smiths, lowering his voice. "I must ask you to be discreet, but we have had several robberies at the hotel recently. Things have been disappearing from rooms – money, jewellery, articles of value. It would have to happen now when we have important guests, even an English lord. "He turned to Harvey. "I offer you the post of guard dog at the hotel."

Harvey cocked his head. He frowned, looking at the Smiths.

"You wish to spend some time with

your new friends?" said Monsieur Emil.
"But that is not a problem. The staff
have been keeping a careful watch dur-
ing the day, however they've seen no
strangers in the hotel. I think the robberies must be happening in the evening
or at night. In the day you are free – at
night you patrol the hotel corridors. I
offer a warm bed in the kitchen and all
the food you can eat. Is it a deal?"

Harvey held out a paw and they shook
hands.

For the next few days the Smiths had the
time of their lives.

Harvey acted as their guide, showing
them around the town. He took Harry
and Sally and Buster swimming and ice-
skating, while Mrs Smith went round
museums and on guided tours and Mr
Smith went to every bank and change

bureau in town comparing their rates
and doing sums on his pocket calculator.

Harvey took them all skiing on the
nursery slopes, showing them the least
crowded ski-lifts and introducing them to
the best instructors. He took them to
back-street restaurants which served
wonderfully inexpensive meals.

Harvey realised the Prior had been
right. He felt much better now he was
being useful. Only one thing spoiled his
happiness – he was having no luck at all
in finding the hotel burglar.

Harvey was worrying about it a few
evenings later as he sat with Mrs Smith
and the three children on the hotel
terrace, after another fun-filled day. They
were waiting for Mr Smith who'd gone off
on some mysterious business of his own.

Tonight, vowed Harvey, he wouldn't
sleep at all. He'd patrol those corridors

right through the night, and if there was a burglar he'd catch him!

"I wish Dad would turn up," said Harry. "I'm starving."

"There he is," said Sally.

Mr Smith bustled up, with an excited air.

"What are you looking so pleased about?" asked Mrs Smith.

"I've got a surprise for you all," said Mr Smith. "You know I've been worrying about changing our money? Well, I've done it – and I've made a real profit. We'll be well off for the rest of the holiday. We'll even have a slap-up meal in Paris on the way home!"

The children all cheered. Mrs Smith looked suspicious – and so did Harvey.

"Oh yes?" said Mrs Smith. "And how did you manage this?"

"You know that chap we met here, that

morning with Harvey?"

"The one Monsieur Emil called Milord?" said Sally.

"That's right. His name's Lord Lummeigh. I ran into him at the bank yesterday. I told him about my problem and he offered to help. Apparently he does a lot of business over here and he can get a special rate."

"John you didn't..."

"Of course not," said Mr Smith. "Do you think I'm silly? I gave him a ten pound cheque – and a few hours later he gave me much more French money than I'd have got at the bank."

"That was yesterday," said Mrs Smith. "What happened today?"

"Well, naturally, I thought it over. This morning I met him again, and I asked him to change the rest of our cheques. He was a bit reluctant at first – apparently it's not strictly legal. I finally managed to persuade him, as a special favour."

Mrs Smith sighed with relief. "You've got the money, then?"

"No, but I will have soon. We arranged to meet here." Mr Smith looked at his watch. "He should have been here by now..."

He realised that everyone – especially

Harvey – was looking reproachfully at him. "It's sure to be all right. He's a guest here. He's a lord! Monsieur Emil knows him..."

Harvey stood up and trotted away. Minutes later he was back with Monsieur Emil, and Mr Smith poured out the whole story. "Wait here please," said Monsieur Emil, and strode away.

They waited in miserable silence until he came back.

"Milord Lummeigh has left us," said Monsieur Emil grimly, "through his bed-room window, without paying his bill. I have spoken to several other guests, and he has kindly helped them to change travellers cheques too, Like you, they are waiting for their money."

He turned to Harvey. "I have also spoken to my staff. Apparently Lord Lummeigh was often seen going into or

coming out of the wrong room. Each time
he explained he was hopelessly absent-
minded and could never remember his
own room number. He was so charming
no-one reported him. No wonder you
didn't catch our burglar, my poor Harvey.

You patrolled the corridors at night – and all the time he was robbing my hotel in broad daylight!"

"He's got all my traveller's cheques," said Mr Smith. "I even signed them for him!"

Harvey hung his head in shame.

He was a total failure, he thought. He'd failed to look after the Smiths and he'd failed as a guard dog. He was useless. All he could do was go back to the monastery, his tail between his legs.

A tear rolled down his nose and splashed to the floor.

## *Chapter Five*
## HARVEY TRIUMPHANT!

It was a sad party that went down to the little station next morning. The Smiths had been forced to cut their holiday short. Monsieur Emil said they could send on the money for their hotel bill when they got home. All they had now was their return tickets and what small change they could rake up between them.

"There'll be no slap-up meal in Paris," said Mr Smith sadly. "We'll be lucky to manage a cup of coffee between us!"

He was plunged in gloom, since the disaster was all his fault.

Harvey too was feeling pretty low. Now the mysterious burglar had escaped with all his loot, Monsieur Emil had no more need for a guard dog. When Harvey had seen off the Smiths he was going back to the monastery – a failure!

At the little station Harry and Sally and Buster all hugged Harvey goodbye. Buster burst into tears when they had to part.

Sadly, Harvey watched them get on the local train that would take them to Paris. Reluctant to set off for the monastery, he lingered to watch the train pull away.

At the very last minute a colourful figure came hurrying past. He wore the leather shorts called *Lederhosen*, an embroidered shirt and a furry green hat with a feather in it, and he was carrying

an enormous rucksack. His face was
brown, not red, his moustache thin and
black, not white and bushy, and his stoop
concealed his height. All the same, he
was Lord Lummeigh – Harvey was sure
of it. There was no deceiving his wonderful bloodhound nose.

The man got on the train just as it was about to leave.

Harvey cleared the station fence with a bound, streaked across the platform and leaped into the guard's van just as the station guard closed the door. The train pulled away.

Harvey spent the rest of the journey wondering what to do next. The trouble with being in the van was that he was trapped there – all he could do was wait.

When the train reached its destination and a guard opened the van door, Harvey leaped over his head and hurried along the platform, eagerly studying the passengers as they descended. He caught a glimpse of the Smiths, though they didn't see him – but the man in Lederhosen with the big rucksack was nowhere to be seen!

Harvey was in despair. He sniffed

hopefully at one possible suspect after another, but it was no good.

Suddenly, a tall man in sports jacket and flannels carrying a suitcase caught his attention. He wore big horn-rimmed glasses and looked pale and weedy, like a teacher on holiday. Immediately, Harvey was back on the scent. He knew at once that this was Lord Lummeigh in yet

another cunning disguise.

Eagerly, Harvey hurried after him.

The man led him across the big station to a special, much more modern-looking section. There were security gates and check-points to be passed but Harvey just bounded over them, ignoring the shouts of the astonished station staff.

Harvey followed his quarry down a

ramp and on to a platform where an amazingly long train stood waiting. Crowds of passengers were climbing on board and suddenly Harvey heard a familiar yell. He hurried forwards and saw the Smith family hauling a struggling Buster on to the train.

"Don' wanna go home!" bellowed Buster.

Harvey followed them on to the train.

It was very crowded and people were working their way along the long open carriages, looking for their reserved seats.

Harvey spotted Mr and Mrs Smith and the children in some seats with a little table between them. Buster was on Mrs Smith's lap, still struggling and yelling.

Harvey trotted up to the table.

"Doggy!" roared Buster delightedly. "Nice doggy!"

Harvey shot under the table and curled up small – or as small as he could!

"Harvey!" said Mr Smith, peering under the table. "What are you doing here? You must get off at once."

"Too late, Dad," said Sally. "We're off!" She was right. The train was sliding smoothly away.

"He can't get off now, there aren't any stops!" said Harry. "We'll just have to hide him and sort things out at the other end." He took off his anorak and draped it over Harvey.

"We can't do that," said Mrs Smith. "It's against the law!"

They were still arguing when the guard came to check their tickets. "A St Bernard dog was running loose on the station and they say it might be on the train. Have you seen it?"

"Er, well..." said Mr Smith.

"We'd certainly have noticed a dog as big as a St Bernard!" said Harry, avoiding the question without actually lying.

"Of course. It's probably just a silly rumour. A St Bernard!" Smiling at such a ridiculous idea, the guard moved on.

Harvey hid under the table for the rest of the journey, which lasted for several hours. Men came down the train checking tickets and passports, but they didn't ask anything about dogs.

Eventually Harvey dropped off to sleep. He was woken up by the familiar sound of the Smiths arguing again.

"Think of all the problems," Mr Smith was saying. "What about quarantine?"

"What about Buster?" said Mrs Smith. "Whenever Harvey's around he's as good as gold!"

"No use arguing about it," said Harry. "We've arrived!"

Harvey realised that the train was slowing down. He wriggled out from under the table and dashed for the train door.

"Harvey, wait! Where are you going?" called Mrs Smith.

Harvey took no notice. He was determined to catch Lord Lummeigh before he got away again. As soon as the door opened. Harvey leaped off the train, dashed to the bottom of the exit ramp and studied the passengers as they came towards him.

A typical British businessman with bowler hat and a big briefcase came hurrying along. At the sight of the big St Bernard looking sternly at him he gasped and then turned and ran.

Harvey bounded after him. The panic-stricken man ran straight into the arms of the Smith family, tripping over Mr Smith's suitcase. He fell, dropping the briefcase, which broke open – spilling out piles of jewellery, money, and travellers cheques!

"My travellers cheques!" shouted Mr Smith, snatching them up.

The man who called himself Lord
Lummeigh tried to run away.

"Bad man!" bellowed Buster, and bit
his ankle.

The man yelled and started to limp off. Harvey barred his way.

"Woof!" said Harvey warningly. The robber stood quite still.

Two policemen came up, attracted by all the fuss.

Mr and Mrs Smith explained about the cheque swindle and the hotel robberies, and the man was handcuffed and taken away.

"Well Harvey," said Sally, "How do you like England?"

Harvey cocked his head in surprise. England?

"That train was the Eurostar," explained Harry. "We've been right through the Channel Tunnel. You're in England now!"

"Woof!" said Harvey, and wagged his tail proudly. He'd caught the robber, he'd helped the Smiths and now he was in a new country. There must be people in England who needed his help!

As a matter of fact there were. Very important people.

But that's another story...